About this book

This book is for everyone who is learning their first words in French. By looking at the little pictures, it will be easy to read and remember the French words underneath.

When you look at the French words, you will see that in front of most of them, there is **le, la, l'** or **les**, which means "the". When you are learning French it is a good idea to learn the **le, la** or **l'** which goes with each one. This is because all words, like bed and table, as well as boy and girl, are masculine or feminine. **Le** means the word is masculine and **la** means it is feminine. When **le** or **la** comes in front of a word beginning with **a, e, i, o, u** or **h**, it usually becomes **l'**. **Les** comes in front of words that are plural; that is when there is more than one, such as beds and tables. **Les** can be either masculine or feminine.

At the back of the book is a guide to help you say all the words in the pictures. But there are some sounds in French which are quite different from any sound in English. To say a French word correctly, you really need to hear a French speaker say it first. Listen very carefully and then try to say it that way yourself. But if you say a word as it is written in the guide, a French person will understand you, even if your French accent is not perfect.

Usborne
First hundred words
in French

Heather Amery
Illustrated by Stephen Cartwright

Translated by Nicole Irving

Edited by Jenny Tyler

Designed by Mike Olley and Jan McCafferty

 There is a little yellow duck to find in every picture.

Le salon   The living room

Papa
Daddy

Maman
Mommy

le garçon
boy

2

la fille
girl

le bébé
baby

le chien
dog

le chat
cat

3

Les vêtements Clothes

les chaussures
shoes

la culotte
underwear

le pull
sweater

le maillot
de corps
undershirt

le pantalon
pants

le tee-shirt
t-shirt

les
chaussettes
socks

Le petit déjeuner Breakfast

le pain
bread

le lait
milk

les oeufs
eggs

la pomme
apple

l'orange
orange

la banane
banana

Dans la cuisine In the kitchen

la table
table

la chaise
chair

l'assiette
plate

8

le couteau
knife

la fourchette
fork

la cuillère
spoon

la tasse
cup

q

Les jouets Toys

le cheval
horse

le mouton
sheep

la vache
cow

la poule
hen

le cochon
pig

le train
train

les cubes
blocks

Chez Grand-mère et Grand-père

Grand-mère
Granny

Grand-père
Grandpa

les pantoufles
slippers

12

At Granny and Grandpa's house

le manteau
coat

la robe
dress

le chapeau
hat

Au jardin public

In the park

l'arbre
tree

la fleur
flower

les balançoires
swings

la balle
ball

14

le toboggan
slide

les bottes
boots

l'oiseau
bird

le bateau
boat

15

Dans la rue In the street

la voiture
car

le vélo
bicycle

l'avion
plane

le camion
truck

l'autobus
bus

la maison
house

La fête The party

le ballon
balloon

le gâteau
cake

la pendule
clock

la glace
ice cream

le poisson
fish

les biscuits
cookies

les bonbons
candy

19

A la piscine
At the swimming pool

le bras
arm

la main
hand

la jambe
leg

les pieds
feet

les orteils
toes

la tête
head

le derrière
bottom

21

Au vestiaire In the changing room

la bouche
mouth

les yeux
eyes

les oreilles
ears

le nez
nose

les cheveux
hair

le peigne
comb

la brosse
brush

Dans le magasin In the store

rouge
red

bleu
blue

vert
green

24

jaune
yellow

rose
pink

blanc
white

noir
black

Dans la salle de bains

In the bathroom

le savon
soap

la serviette
towel

les toilettes
toilet

26

le bain
bathtub

le ventre
tummy

le canard
duck

Dans la chambre
In the bedroom

le lit
bed

la lampe
lamp

la fenêtre
window

la porte
door

le livre
book

la poupée
doll

l'ours
teddy bear

Match the words to the pictures

la balle

la banane

les bottes

le canard

le chapeau

le chat

les chaussettes

le chien

le cochon

le couteau

la fenêtre

la fourchette

le gâteau

la glace

le lait

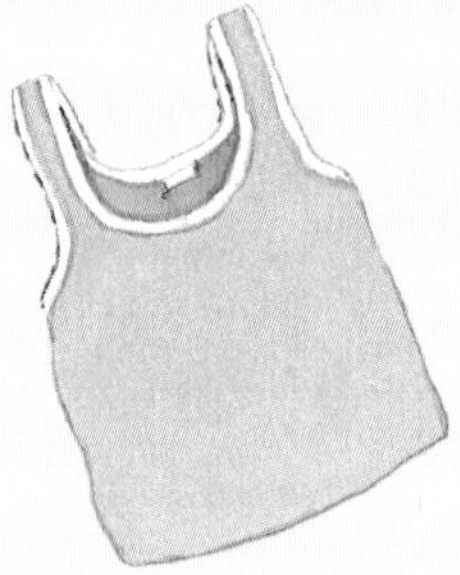

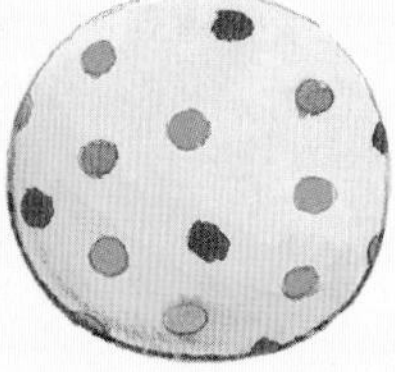

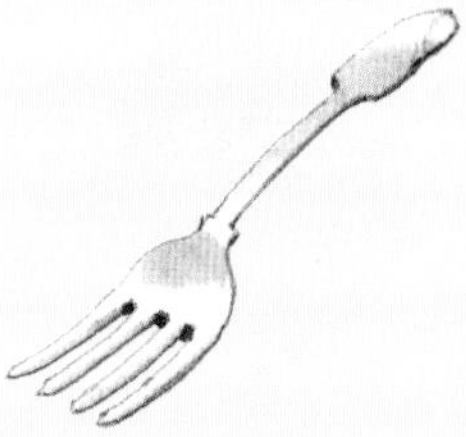

la lampe

le livre

le maillot
de corps

l'oeuf

l'orange

l'ours

la pendule

le poisson

la pomme

la poupée

le pull

la table

le train

la vache

la voiture

Les nombres Numbers

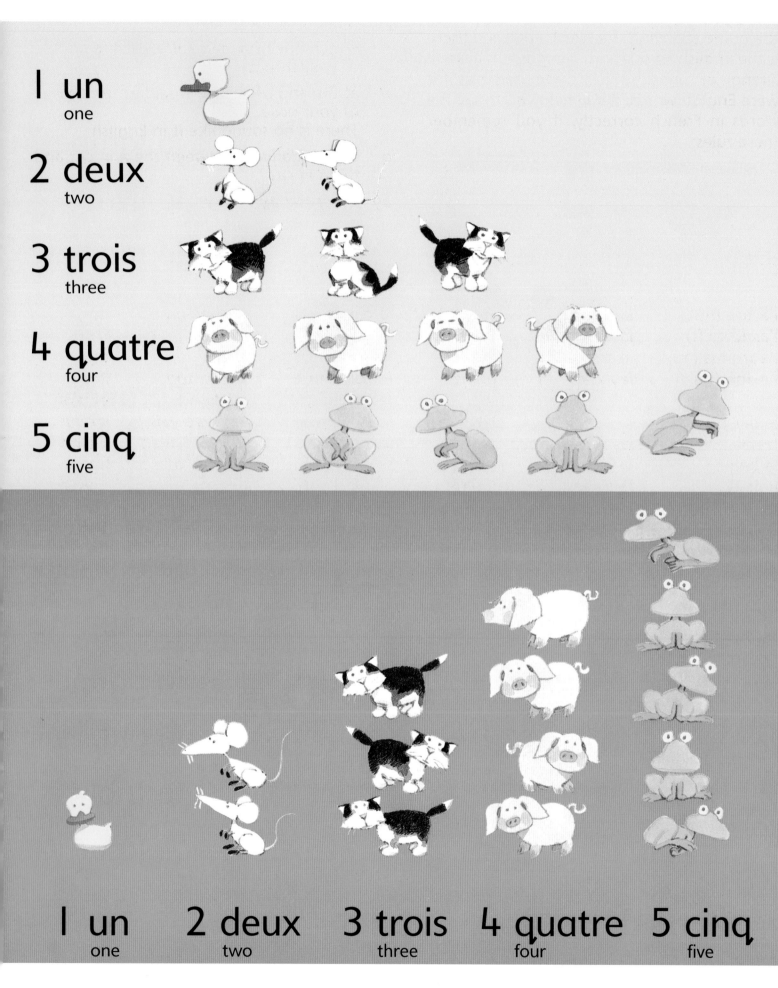

1 un
one

2 deux
two

3 trois
three

4 quatre
four

5 cinq
five

1 un
one

2 deux
two

3 trois
three

4 quatre
four

5 cinq
five

Words in the pictures

In this alphabetical list of all the words in the pictures, the French word comes first, next is the guide to saying the word, and then there is the English translation. The guide may look strange or funny, but just try to read it as if it were English words. It will help you to say the words in French correctly, if you remember these rules:

g is said like **g** in **g**ame

j is said like **s** in trea**s**ure

r is made by growling a little at the back of your throat

n at the end of a word is said at the back of your nose.
There is no sound like it in English

a sounds halfway between the **a** in c**a**t and the **a** in c**a**r

ay is like the **ay** in d**ay**

French	Guide	English
l'arbre (m)	*lar-br*	tree
l'assiette (f)	*lass-ee-et*	plate
l'autobus (m)	*lo-toe-bews*	bus
l'avion (m)	*lav-yon*	plane
le bain	*le ban*	bathtub
les balançoires (f)	*lay bal-on-swar*	swings
la balle	*la bal*	ball
le ballon	*le ba-lon*	balloon
la banane	*la ba-nan*	banana
le bateau	*le ba-toe*	boat
le bébé	*le bay-bay*	baby
les biscuits (m)	*lay beess-kwee*	cookies
blanc	*blon*	white
bleu	*bler*	blue
les bonbons (m)	*lay bon-bon*	candy
les bottes (f)	*lay bot*	boots
la bouche	*la boosh*	mouth
le bras	*le bra*	arm
la brosse	*la bross*	brush
le camion	*le ka-mee-on*	truck
le canard	*le ka-nar*	duck
la chaise	*la shayz*	chair
la chambre	*la shom-br*	bedroom
le chapeau	*le sha-poe*	hat
le chat	*le sha*	cat
les chaussettes (f)	*lay show-set*	socks
les chaussures (f)	*lay show-sewr*	shoes
le cheval	*le sher-val*	horse
les cheveux (m)	*lay sher-ver*	hair
le chien	*le shee-an*	dog
cinq	*sank*	five
le cochon	*le cosh-on*	pig
le couteau	*le coo-toe*	knife
les cubes (m)	*lay kewb*	blocks
la cuillère	*la kwee-yair*	spoon
la cuisine	*la kwee-zeen*	kitchen
la culotte	*la kew-lot*	under-wear
le derrière	*le dare-ee-air*	bottom
deux	*der*	two
la fenêtre	*la fe-netr*	window
la fête	*la fet*	party
la fille	*la fee-ye*	girl
la fleur	*la fler*	flower
la fourchette	*la foor-shet*	fork
le garçon	*le gar-sonn*	boy
le gâteau	*le ga-toe*	cake
la glace	*la glass*	ice cream
Grand-mère	*gron-mair*	Granny
Grand-père	*gron-pair*	Grandpa
la jambe	*la jomb*	leg
le jardin public	*le jar-dan poo-bleek*	park
jaune	*jone*	yellow
les jouets (m)	*lay joo-ay*	toys

33

le lait	*le lay*	milk	la porte	*la por-t*	door
la lampe	*la lomp*	lamp	la poule	*la pool*	hen
le lit	*le lee*	bed	la poupée	*la poo-pay*	doll
le livre	*le lee-vr*	book	le pull	*le pewl*	sweater
le magasin	*le ma-ga-zan*	store	quatre	*ka-tr*	four
le maillot de corps	*le my-o de cor*	under-shirt	la robe	*la rob*	dress
la main	*la man*	hand	rose	*rose*	pink
la maison	*la may-zon*	house	rouge	*rooj*	red
Maman	*ma-mon*	Mommy	la rue	*la roo*	street
le manteau	*le mon-toe*	coat			
le mouton	*le moo-ton*	sheep	la salle de bains	*la sal-de-ban*	bathroom
			le salon	*le salon*	living room
le nez	*le nay*	nose			
noir	*nwar*	black	le savon	*le sa-von*	soap
les nombres (m)	*lay nom-br*	numbers	la serviette	*la sair-vee-et*	towel
l'oeuf (m)	*lerf*	egg	la table	*la ta-bl*	table
les oeufs (m)	*lay zer*	eggs	la tasse	*la tass*	cup
l'oiseau (m)	*lwa-zoe*	bird	le tee-shirt	*le tee-shirt*	t-shirt
l'orange (f)	*lor-onj*	orange	la tête	*la tet*	head
les oreilles (f)	*lay zor-ay*	ears	le toboggan	*le tob-og-on*	slide
les orteils (m)	*lay zor-tay*	toes	les toilettes (f)	*lay twal-et*	toilet
l'ours (m)	*loorce*	teddy bear	le train	*le tran*	train
			trois	*trwa*	three
le pain	*le pan*	bread	un	*an*	one
le pantalon	*le pon-ta-lon*	pants			
les pantoufles (f)	*lay pon-too-fl*	slippers	la vache	*la vash*	cow
Papa	*pa-pa*	Daddy	le vélo	*le vay-lo*	bicycle
le peigne	*le payn-ye*	comb	le ventre	*le von-tr*	tummy
la pendule	*la pon-dewl*	clock	vert	*vair*	green
le petit déjeuner	*le pe-tee day-je-nay*	breakfast	le vestiaire	*le vays-tee-air*	changing room
les pieds (m)	*lay pee-ay*	feet	les vêtements (m)	*lay vet-mon*	clothes
la piscine	*la pee-seen*	swimming pool	la voiture	*la vwa-tewr*	car
le poisson	*le pwa-sonn*	fish	les yeux (m)	*layz-yer*	eyes
la pomme	*la pomm*	apple			

This edition first published in 2001 by Usborne Publishing Ltd, Usborne House, 83-85 Saffron Hill, London EC1N 8RT, England.
www.usborne.com
Copyright © 2001, 1988 Usborne Publishing Ltd.